To: Abley

From: Denny -"Bea-Bea"
   & Garland

Feb. 26-2015

This book belongs to

_____

_____

For all our great-nephews and nieces
T.B.-B. & J.B.-B.

This edition published by Parragon Books Ltd in 2014 and distributed by

Parragon Inc.
440 Park Avenue South, 13th Floor
New York, NY 10016
www.parragon.com

ISBN 978-1-4723-8585-7

Printed in China

My Favorite Food

Tiziana & John Bendall-Brunello

PaRragon

Bath · New York · Cologne · Melbourne · Delhi
Hong Kong · Shenzhen · Singapore · Amsterdam

Little Goose and her mommy were in the yard, enjoying some fresh, green grass.

"Mmm . . . I love grass," said Little Goose. "It's my favorite food!

I wonder if everybody loves grass as much as me?"

"Why don't you go and find out," said Mommy.

So off went Little Goose to find out Pig's favorite food . . .

"What's your favorite food, Pig?"
she asked.

"Apples,"

said Pig. "They're so juicy!"

"Mmm," said Little Goose, "I like apples too.
I wonder what Goat's favorite food is?"

So off she went to find out . . .

"What's your favorite food, Goat?"
asked Little Goose.

"Socks,"
said Goat. "They're so chewy!"

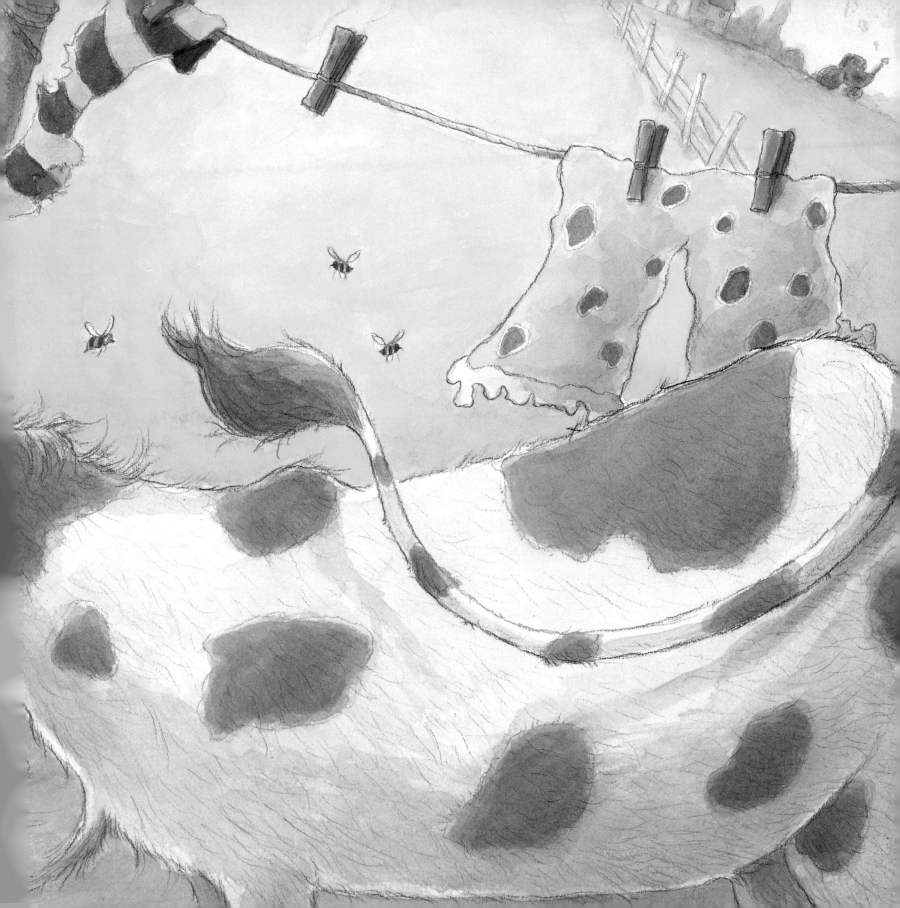

"Hmmm," said Little Goose,
"I'm not sure I like socks!

I wonder what Cow's favorite food is?"

So off she went to find out . . .

"What's your favorite food, Cow?" asked Little Goose.

"Daisies," said Cow. "They're so sweet!"

"Mmm," said Little Goose, "daisies are tasty.
But I wonder what Fox's
favorite food is?"

So off she went to find out . . .

"Fox! Fox! What's your favorite food?" asked Little Goose.

"Well . . ." said Fox,
"let me think.
My favorite food is . . ."

"YOU!"

"Yikes!" squealed Little Goose.
And she ran away as fast as her
little legs would carry her . . .

. . . safely back into
the loving wings
of her mommy.

And while Little Goose enjoyed some of her
favorite food—grass—

Fox settled down to eat his favorite food—**strawberries!**